The characters and events in this book are fictitious. Any similarity to real persons, living or dead, is coincidental and not intended by the authors.

Front cover and all illustrations by Dora Hegedus

CAT WORLD!

FREEZE'S ADVENTURE

WRITTEN BY MARCUS AND SETH WEISEL

ILLUSTRATIONS BY DORA HEGEDUS

Our Story (About Telling Stories)

Every morning, my son Marcus and I go out for a walk, scooter, or bike ride, and during the ride we tell a story. At first, I decided I was the storyteller. I would try to make up a story, often to try to teach a lesson. Naturally, he hated it! He kept trying to jump in to change the story. I quickly realized how great it was. We settled into a good rhythm where we each took turns telling parts of the story.

From the beginning, the stories all seemed to be about cats. Sometimes a story lasts a day, sometimes a month or more. By now, we've created an entire world of cats and their stories. Marcus is truly the author, and I'm essentially the editor. Our amazing illustrator, Dora Hegedus has helped bring them to life. A child's sense of whimsy and adventure is what Cat World! is all about. We hope you enjoy reading Cat World! as much as we've enjoying creating it!

Table of Contents

Chapter 1

Off to the Beach

One morning, Freeze and his mommy and daddy were packing up snacks and toys to bring to the beach.

"Oh, and I definitely want to bring this one," said Freeze as he picked up a toy dinosaur.

Freeze is a kitten. Yes, his name is actually Freeze! You might be curious why Freeze is named Freeze. Well, it's because he often goes out in very cold weather and freezes.

But don't worry, it doesn't bother him very much. Freeze and his family were going to meet some of Freeze's friends, who were also kittens, at the beach. Freeze was excited about his big day at the beach.

Little did he know he'd have a much bigger adventure ahead of him than just going to the beach. Before the end of his adventure, he would drive a car transporter across the ocean floor, take a long road trip to visit his grandparents, get stuck in a huge storm, and become frozen in garbage... on Pluto. But he didn't know any of that yet!

"OK, let's go!" said Freeze's daddy.

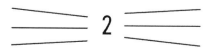

Freeze and his family were packed and ready to go, so Freeze's daddy drove the family to the beach. Freeze's daddy didn't drive a normal car. He didn't drive an SUV either. He didn't drive a pick-up truck, a sports car, or anything like that. Instead, he drove a car transporter. While that might seem like an odd choice, it made perfect sense to Freeze since his daddy drove a car transporter for his job.

On the drive to the beach, Freeze was looking out of the window.

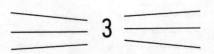

"Daddy, look!" Freeze shouted as he pointed to a car on the side of the road.

"Flat tire!" said Freeze.

"Thanks Freeze!" said his daddy.

Freeze's daddy pulled over to the side of the road and loaded the car with the flat tire onto the car transporter. Soon after that, there was a broken-down car on the side of the road, so they stopped to pick up that car too. Then they drove both cars to the auto mechanic so he could fix them. Sure, the drive took a bit longer than they expected, but it was Freeze's daddy's job!

Eventually they got to the beach. They looked and looked for parking but couldn't find any open spots. It was a very busy day at the beach.

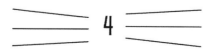

"Daddy, I have an idea. Since there are no open parking spots, maybe we can drive right onto the beach and park there!" said Freeze.

"Great idea, Freeze!" said Daddy.

There were no roads on the beach, so they had to drive right on the sand.

Freeze's daddy wasn't used to driving on the sand, and he lost control of the car transporter! He swerved and swayed and slid and spun.

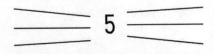

"Look out!" yelled Freeze.

The transporter crashed into a grill and caught on fire! The cats jumped out of the transporter, threw hot dogs and hamburgers out of their way, and yelled for the fireman to come. While they waited, Freeze ate all of the hot dogs and sausages that weren't covered with sand.

One minute later, a firetruck came by. The fireman quickly connected the hose to the fire hydrant on the street.

The firetruck was too far from the car transporter, so the hose couldn't reach the fire! The fireman used a fire helicopter instead. The fire helicopter filled up a giant bucket with ocean water and poured the water on the transporter to put out the fire.

Chapter 2

The Most Dangerous Game

"Phew!" said Freeze. "Now we can play!"

With the fire safely put out, Freeze and his parents started to play by the water. They had brought a lot of toys with them.

"Which toy do you want to play with, Freezie?" asked Mommy.

"Umm, I can't decide. I think I'll just play with all of them," said Freeze.

Freeze jumped right into the bag and grabbed every single toy there. They played with a shovel, a bucket, a rake, a firetruck, a police car, a mini car transporter, a dinosaur... and about 1,000 other toys. After having some fun with the toys, Freeze came up with a new game.

"Let's put a toy in the ocean and see what happens," said Freeze.

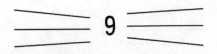

"Ok," said Mommy. "Just be careful you don't lose your toys."

He put his shovel into the water and grabbed it before it floated away.

"That was fun!" said Freeze.

Then he put a few other toys in the ocean and grabbed those before they floated away.

"That was even more fun!" said Freeze.

Finally, he put all 1,000 toys into the ocean.

"Freezie wait!" said Mommy.

But it was too late! A huge wave came and swept the toys away. Freeze tried to grab them, but there were too many to collect. The toys started to float away!

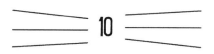

"My toys!" screamed Freeze.

"Be careful Freezie!" shouted Mommy.

"Save the T-Rex!" yelled Daddy.

Meanwhile, Freeze's friends, Hike, Pool, and Cold, were already at the beach, playing by the water.

"I love the cold water," said Cold.

"I love all the trails by the beach... not to mention all the animals," said Hike.

Then Pool said, "And I just love being by the water! It's so calm and—"

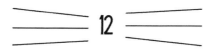

Suddenly, they heard Freeze and his parents screaming about the toys and ran over to help. None of the kittens could swim so all they could do was yell as the toys floated farther and farther away.

Just then, they saw Beach swimming. Beach was another one of their cat friends. He was a great swimmer. In fact, he swam across the Atlantic Ocean to Portugal every day.

BEEEACH!!

"Beach!!! Beeeeach!!! BEEEEEACH!!!"
The kittens yelled as loud as they could.

He heard them! He looked around and noticed the toys floating everywhere. He was able to get all of the toys that were floating. But many of them had already sunk underwater.

"What are we going to do now?!" cried Freeze.

Ocean Drive

Freeze was feeling very sad about losing his toys.

"There are so many toys that sunk into the ocean," he said. "I wish we could go down there and scoop them all up... Wait, that's it!" he shouted.

"What is it?" asked Hike.

"We can drive the car transporter into the ocean to collect the toys!" answered Freeze.

Freeze and his friends jumped into the car transporter and drove it right into the ocean! They drove across the ocean floor. It was incredible. They saw lots of interesting animals including sea turtles, sharks, and a crocodile!

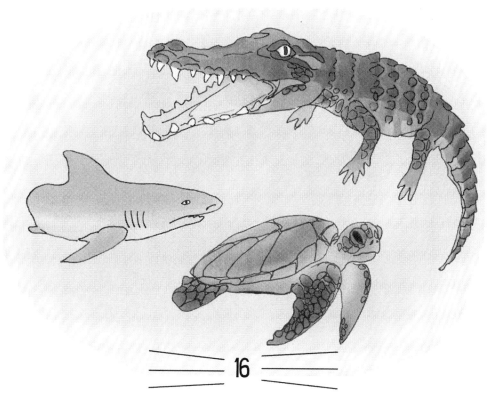

"What's that?" asked Pool, as he pointed out the window.

"Hmmm – I don't know, but it's big and it's getting closer to us," said Cold.

"I know what that is – it's a blue whale!" said Hike.

It was huge! The kittens stared at the giant whale. The whale was curious about the car transporter and started to swim right toward them.

"Wow, we're getting so close," said Pool.

"Too close," said Freeze. "We're going to crash!"

Freeze turned wildly to avoid the giant animal.

"Aaaaaaaaaaahh!!!" they all screamed, as they barely made it past the whale. They started to tip over from the sharp turn!

"We're going to flip!" yelled Pool.

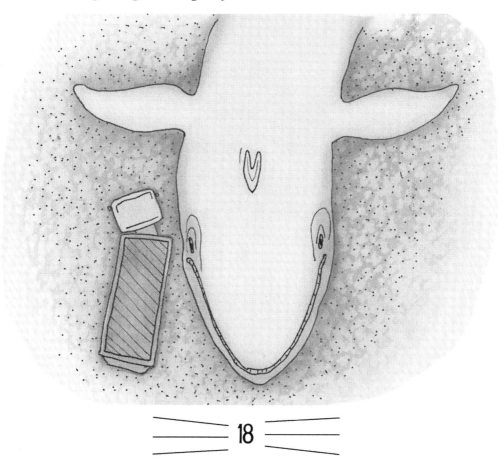

"Quick, everyone run to the other side of the transporter to balance the weight," screamed Freeze.

It was working. The car transporter was coming back down. But just when they thought they might be ok, a powerful underwater tidal wave knocked them over. The kittens were knocked out of the car transporter and floated to the ocean surface!

"Now we'll never find the toys," said Pool.

"And we lost the car transporter!" added Cold.

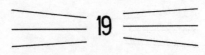

As if that weren't bad enough, the kittens were suddenly stung by a stingray! And a jellyfish!

Floating on the water, hurting and feeling sad, the kittens heard a loud noise.

"What was that?" asked Hike.

"It's a motorboat!" answered Pool.

Wrong Way!

"Quick, let's get his attention," Hike suggested.

They waved their arms, and the boat came along and picked up the kittens.

"Thanks for picking us up," said Hike.

"My pleasure," said the cat driver. "My name is Motorboat."

After that quick hello, Motorboat started driving the boat. The kittens were so happy that they were safe.

"Wow – this boat is fast!" said Hike.

"And LOUD!" added Pool.

"Where are we going?" Cold asked Motorboat, but Motorboat didn't hear him.

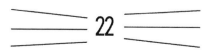

Cold tried again, this time even louder. "WHERE ARE WE GOING?"

Motorboat still couldn't hear Cold's question.

The other cats shouted to Motorboat to tell him that they needed to go back to the beach, but he couldn't hear them because he was too focused, and the motor was too loud.

"I think we're going the wrong way!" said Hike.

Then the boat hit a water ramp that sent the boat high in the air and then splashing back down into the water!

Hike, Cold, and Pool were so focused on the motorboat that they didn't notice that Freeze wasn't on the motorboat. In fact, Freeze had not floated up to the surface with the rest of the kittens. He was still down at the bottom of the ocean, trying to fix the car transporter. When he finished rebuilding it, he pushed it to the shore.

Mommy and daddy were still at the beach, staring at the water, wondering when the kittens were going to come back. They saw something far out in the water.

"Is that a boat?" asked Mommy.

"Could it be a car?" responded Daddy.

When they looked closely, they could see that the driver had whiskers.

"Who could that be?" asked Mommy.

Then they recognized that cat and said, "Freeze, you're here!"

They couldn't believe it. But where were the other kittens?

Meanwhile, back on the motorboat, the kittens kept trying to yell to the driver, but it was no use. The boat was too loud.

"Look up there!" Cold shouted as he pointed to an airplane nearby.

He jumped up and down and waved his hands.

Hike and Pool did the same. "We're here!" they shouted together.

The driver of the airplane saw them and flew down very low and close to the motorboat. The kittens jumped right onto the airplane from the motorboat.

"Take us to the beach, please," they asked the pilot.

It only took one minute for the airplane to bring them back to the beach. At the beach, Cold, Hike, and Pool saw Freeze. They were so happy to be back together.

Chapter 5

Finding Tires with Tire

"Check out what I did," said Freeze as he showed them the car transporter.

"Wow – you fixed the car transporter," said Pool. "Let's drive back into the ocean to pick up the rest of the toys."

But the other cats were worried that they might crash again. It was time for a new plan.

"I have an idea!" announced Freeze. "My grandparents took me fishing once. We used a fishing rod to catch fish from deep in the ocean. Maybe we can fish for the toys!" he explained. "We can drive the car transporter to my grandparent's house, borrow the fishing rod, drive back to the ocean, and fish for all the toys."

"That's a great plan, Freeze," said Hike. "Let's do it! But first, let's stop at the tiki hut, and eat some french fries," he added.

"I can't say no to that," answered Freeze.

After eating the yummy french fries, they started to drive the car transporter. Soon after they started driving, they heard a funny sound coming from the car transporter.

They got out to look at the tires. One tire was missing! It turned out that it had rolled all the way to Albania. There was no way they could get that tire back, so they needed to get a new tire.

While the cats were staring at the missing wheel, a Jeep came by, and the driver got out. "Hi, my name is Tire," he said. "I see you have a missing tire. Don't worry. I have a spare!"

They tried to put the tire on the car transporter, but it did not fit. It was too big!

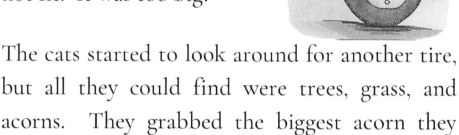

The cats started to look around for another tire, but all they could find were trees, grass, and acorns. They grabbed the biggest acorn they could find – it was huge!

Freeze worked hard to turn it into an acorn wheel, but it was too small and didn't work.

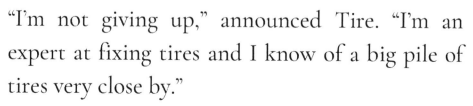

"I'm not giving up," announced Tire. "I'm an expert at fixing tires and I know of a big pile of tires very close by."

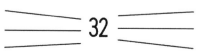

They went with Tire to the pile of tires, but they were all too big. They needed a small one! But not as small as the acorn. They were going to have to get creative.

"What if we make a tire out of a pile of leaves?" asked Pool.

"Brilliant, let's do it!" answered Tire.

They collected all of the leaves they could find and made them into a huge ball. It was perfect. But then the wind came and blew them all away!

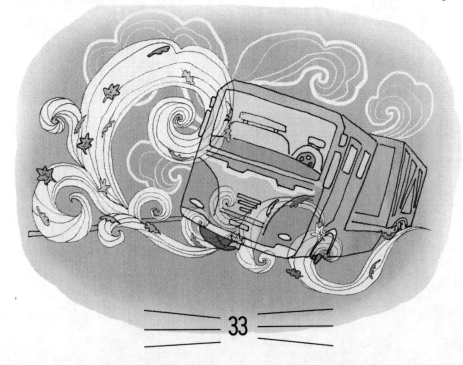

The next day, they tried again. "The leaves didn't work," said Freeze. "Any other ideas?" he asked.

"I've got it!" said Pool. "What if we put the leaves into a bag?"

"That's it!" said Tire.

But the bag flew away too, because it was too light! The cats were feeling discouraged.

Suddenly, Freeze started to look for things to use inside the car transporter and in all of the cars that were on the car transporter. They made a tire out of a ball with tape, glue, and magnets. It worked! They were back on track. Off to Grandma and Grandpa's house!

The Hurricane

The cats drove the car transporter all the way from Virginia to Pennsylvania. Along the way they took lots of stops, had lots of snacks and drinks, did lots of reading, and played games. Finally, they made it to Grandpa and Grandma's house in Pennsylvania.

Ding-Dong! They rang the bell.

Grandma and Grandpa were so surprised and happy to see them. They played and read. Whenever Grandpa drank something, the kittens and Freeze jumped up, because they knew they were going to get a sip of it too! They were so happy they decided to stay for 1,000 years!

The day after Freeze, Cold, Pool, and Hike got to Grandma and Grandpa's house, the doorbell rang. It was Mommy and Daddy!

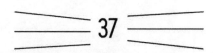

"Mommy and Daddy! What are you doing here?" asked Freeze.

"We were worried about you driving in the car transporter all by yourselves, so we found a new car and followed you to Grandma and Grandpa's house," they explained. "But we can't stay long. We're going on vacation to a wedding for a week. Grandma and Grandpa will babysit you and the kittens."

Then it was dinnertime and Grandma made dinner. Grandpa was reading with the kittens and Freeze. Grandma made a healthy salad for dinner. The kittens did not like that! Grandma made a deal with them that if they ate the whole salad, they could have ice cream and cookies for dessert.

The kittens ate some, but not all of their dinner. Grandma decided they could have the cookies. Then Freeze and the kittens asked for ice cream too, but Grandma said, "no way!"

After dinner it was time for bed, but the kittens were not tired. They played under the blanket and were very energetic. They played all night!!

The night lasted forever. It was very late when Freeze and the kittens heard a loud BOOM!

"What was that?" asked Pool.

They were scared. They ran to the window and saw that it was raining. There was a big storm!

Soon there was a flash of lightning. CRACK!

"Did you see that?" asked Hike.

And more thunder. BOOM!!

Then they heard a strange noise outside.

"Did you hear that?" asked Cold.

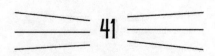

Then the power went off! It was completely dark inside the house. Even the nightlight went off.

Grandma and Grandpa came by to check on the kittens.

"We heard something out in the yard, so we're going to go out for a quick look," they explained.

When they stepped outside, the wind was so strong that they got lifted into the air for a second!

"Back inside!" yelled Grandpa as they ran back into the house.

They were very tired from being out in the storm, but they had to go back outside, because they had to go to the airport.

"Ok, kittens. You'll be on your own for a little while because we need to go to the airport for our vacation now. We've left you plenty of food and milk and water. Bye!" said Grandma and Grandpa as they waved goodbye.

Grandma and Grandpa went outside and were getting soaked when finally, a car came and brought them to the airport. Their flight was delayed for a long time because of the hurricane. They had lots of extra time, so they ate some food in the airport.

Frozen Garbage

The kittens were all alone in the dark house!

"So... what do we do now?" asked Pool.

"I think I saw some toys outside," said Hike. "Let's go get them!"

"I'm not sure that's a good idea," said Freeze. "What about the storm?"

"We'll be fine!" said Cold.

They went outside. As soon as they got outside, the wind launched the cats right into the air!

In the air, Freeze got pooped on by a seagull. And then the other kittens got pooped on too!

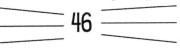

The kittens and Freeze were getting very cold and scared, flying in the air in the big storm.

"What do we do now?" asked Pool.

"I don't know," answered Freeze. "Maybe we can grab onto a tree and climb back down?"

But just then, a huge gust of wind blew them all the way to Pluto! Grandma and Grandpa were in the airplane and saw Freeze and the kittens being blown into space. They couldn't believe it!

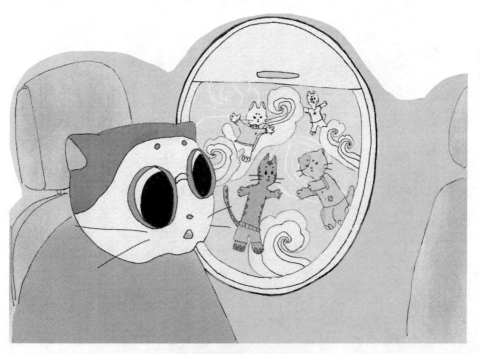

The kittens and Freeze landed on Pluto, and it was super cold.

"I think I'm going to freeze," said Hike.

"No, I'm Freeze," said Freeze. "I'm so cold!"

"No, I'm Cold," said Cold.

"No, I'm really starting to freeze," said Hike.

It was true! It was so cold that they all started to freeze. Soon they froze into big blocks of ice. They couldn't move! Suddenly, they felt like they were moving, but they couldn't understand why. They realized that a Gigantosaurus was pushing them!

"Ahhhhh!!! It's a space dinosaur!!" Freeze tried to scream.

But since he was frozen, all he could really say was "Mmmm!!! Mmm mm mm mmm-mm-mmmm!!"

The Gigantosaurus was huge and so scary. But he didn't try to eat them. Instead, he pushed them and knocked them over. He rolled the frozen catsicles right into a garbage can. It was so stinky! Finally, the Gigantosaurus left them alone.

They were so happy that he left, but they were not alone for long. Just then, the Big Bad Wolf pushed the garbage can that they were in into another garbage can! It was even stinker!

Then it was quiet and still. Suddenly, it felt like they were moving again.

A hippopotamus pushed those garbage cans right into another garbage can! What was happening!?!

Then the Pluto garbage man came and put them all into the garbage truck. It was super stinky! The truck brought them to the dump. It was the stinkiest of all!

Chapter 8

Break the Ice

Meanwhile, Grandma and Grandpa landed in Madagascar.

"Grandpa, as much as I want to take this vacation in Madagascar, we need to help the kittens!" said Grandma.

"I agree!" said Grandpa. "Let's get on the next flight!"

But first, since they had some time before their flight, they ate another meal in the airport. Then they got into a race car spaceship and flew right away to Pluto. The trip was very fast.

When they landed on Pluto, they walked to the dump and saw the big blocks of ice.

"Look over there!" yelled Grandma.

Grandpa took a hammer from his fanny pack and smashed the ice!

"I see whiskers poking through the ice!" shouted Grandpa.

"Let's keep smashing the ice!" Grandma shouted back.

After breaking off more of the ice, they could see a whole cat's face.

"It's Freeze!" said Grandma.

They finished removing the ice from Freeze and the kittens! They were so excited to see each other. The kittens crawled all over Grandma and Grandpa. They got into the race car spaceship and flew to their house right away. It was so good to get home. So cozy.

Then the kittens asked, "when are Mommy and Daddy going to come?"

"Two million billion years!" joked Grandpa.

Mommy and Daddy had gone on a big trip to a wedding. When they were driving home, they got stuck in the same big storm as Grandma, Grandpa, and the kittens. It was a huge storm. It covered all of the planets, except Mars.

There was so much rain that the roads had flooded. Then they ran out of gas and had a flat tire. Luckily, they were able to pump up the tire, and a gas helicopter filled them up with gas. Finally, they were able to drive home.

Ding-dong! rang the doorbell. Freeze and the kittens ran to the door and shouted together, "Who is it?"

"It's Mommy and Daddy!" they answered. "Let us in!"

Mommy and Daddy went inside and hugged Freeze and the kittens. It had been a crazy adventure for everyone. They were all so happy to be back together. But they were also so tired. They all went to bed and fell asleep right away.

Epilogue

The next day, Freeze, the kittens, Mommy, Daddy, Grandma, and Grandpa woke up. They put on their clothes and ate some breakfast. Grandpa ate cereal, Freeze and the kittens ate fish, and Grandma, Mommy, and Daddy ate oatmeal with blueberries and strawberries. After breakfast, Freeze and the kittens played quietly while Grandma meditated.

"The beach toys!" said Freeze. "We never picked up the rest! Daddy, can you please drive us back to the beach? Please?" he begged.

"I don't think so Freeze," answered Daddy.

"Pleeeaase?" asked Freeze.

"Well....." said Daddy.

"Pleeeeeeeaaaaaaaase???" asked Freeze.

"Ah, okay! Let's go!" said Daddy.

When they got to the beach, they saw that their friend Beach was already there. Beach taught them how to drive a taxi boat.

He was a great teacher and soon the kittens were driving the taxi boat!

They drove all around the ocean and used Grandma and Grandpa's fishing rod to pick up all of the beach toys that they lost so long ago! They played with the beach toys... on the beach, all day, and then went back home.

The End?

KIDDING!!!
KEEP READING FOR MORE CAT WORLD!

SHOP'S ADVENTURE

Sign up for our newsletter and receive a **free** copy of Shop's Adventure!

HTTPS://CATWORLDBOOKS.COM

Did you love Freeze's Adventure? Leave a review on Amazon to help spread the word! Just a sentence or two is greatly appreciated!

About the Authors and Illustrator

Marcus Weisel loves food even more than he loves telling stories. He also really loves cats, dinosaurs, and outer space.

Seth Weisel is a very proud dad. He too loves cats, dinosaurs, and outer space. Seth, his wife Eva, and their son Marcus, have recently moved to Florida where they are searching for alligators.

Dora Hegedus also shares a love for cats! She is also proud to help visualize Marcus's story. Continuing on with her studies, she will be finishing university soon!

The Cats of Cat World!

1. **Banana** - loves to eat bananas and any fruit
2. **Banana Pancake** - loves to eat bananas, pancakes, and banana pancakes
3. **Beach** - loves to swim. Swims from New York to Portugal every day. It takes 100 hours and 60 minutes.
4. **Berry** - loves to eat berries
5. **Box** - loves to climb into boxes
6. **Bus** - loves to ride on the bus in the city
7. **Cold** - loves cold weather and has white fur
8. **Cranky** - is always cranky
9. **Dinosaur** - likes to find great fossils of dinosaurs. Also loves to find out mysteries about dinosaurs in museums
10. **Dinosaur Time** - lives in the time of dinosaurs. Loves dinosaurs
11. **Fence** - loves to jump over fences
12. **Food** - loves to eat
13. **Freeze** - is very often frozen
14. **Grumpy** - is always grumpy

The Cats of Cat World!

15. **Halloween** - loves Halloween and getting dressed up in a costume
16. **Hike** - loves to hike. Can also find his way back if he gets lost.
17. **Hot** - is always hot. Sometimes he burns.
18. **Jail** - lives in jail
19. **Long Drive** - loves long drives
20. **Mall** - really likes to go to malls
21. **Medium Drive** - loves medium drives
22. **Motorboat** - drives a motorboat
23. **Mountain** - loves to be on mountains. Sometimes falls onto the ground.
24. **Plant** - loves plants. Sometimes even gets in danger because he goes into a Venus fly trap
25. **Pool** - loves to swim, especially in a pool
26. **Quiet** - is always quiet
27. **Rain** - loves to get wet and go out in the rain, even in a hurricane, which sometimes gets him into trouble
28. **Ride** - loves to ride all vehicles

The Cats of Cat World!

29. **Rock** - loves to hide inside rocks. Friends with Tree.
30. **Run** - loves to run everywhere
31. **Shadow** - loves any shadow
32. **Shop** - loves to go to stores and restaurants to eat. Sometimes swims in giant peanut jars and eats the peanuts.
33. **Short Drive** - loves short drives
34. **Shout** - loves to be loud. Super loud.
35. **Slow Down** - is always telling everyone else to slow down
36. **Smoothie** - loves to drink smoothies. Loves all smoothies except broccoli and avocado.
37. **Space** - lives in a space station
38. **Taco** - loves to eat tacos. Friends with Shop and Food.
39. **Tag** - loves to play tag
40. **The Kittens** - thousands of kittens who all go places together

The Cats of Cat World!

41. **Tire** - loves tires. Uses them to help people and to fight bad guys. He is the smallest cat.
42. **Tree** - loves to climb up trees. Expert at climbing up, but is too scared to come down. Sometimes tries, and falls and crashes
43. **Ugo** - leader of the cats. Always telling cats what they should do.
44. **Walk** - loves to walk
45. **What** - always says "what?"

...and many more that we couldn't remember!

Cat Universe and Stinky Butt World

Cat Universe!

Marcus and I have told some more complicated "big kid" stories that happen on other planets and with time travel. The kittens Dinosaur Time and Space are technically part of Cat Universe, though they do appear in Cat World stories.

We may one day expand to write these stories as part of Cat Universe! These would be for older readers (ages 7-8, according to Marcus).

Stinky Butt World!

Some of the stories that we've told are too violent, gross, or weird for Cat World! These are the stories of Stinky Butt World! Marcus thinks these are the best stories of all time.

Some of the cats in Stinky Butt World include Lava Pants, Tornado Shirt, Drool Boogers, Burp Cough, Fartenstein, and of course, Stinky Butt.

Now It's Your Turn

Congratulations, you've finished reading our story! Now go out and start telling stories together. Seriously, do it. We're not kidding. Do it! Don't just smile and put the book down. Start telling stories! Ok, you can start tomorrow morning if it's bedtime right now.

Made in the USA
Monee, IL
23 December 2024

75280938R00044